A Loon Alone

By Pamela Love

Illustrated by Shannon Sycks

Cover and interior design by Lindy Gifford

6   5

ISBN 978-0-89272-526-7

Library of Congress Control Number 2001096774

BOOKS·MAGAZINE·ONLINE
w w w . d o w n e a s t . c o m

OGPHK
Printed in China
Manufactuer's Information
O.G. Printing Productions, Ltd.
Kowloon, Hong Kong
October 2010

To my husband, Andrew; my son, Robert;
and my parents, Ray and Jean Gibson

On a lake in the Maine woods, two loons—a mother and chick—were swimming together. Usually, the chick kept close to his mother.

But sometimes, he would dive and bring up a smooth, white stone in his dark gray bill. It was play—but also practice for catching fish someday.

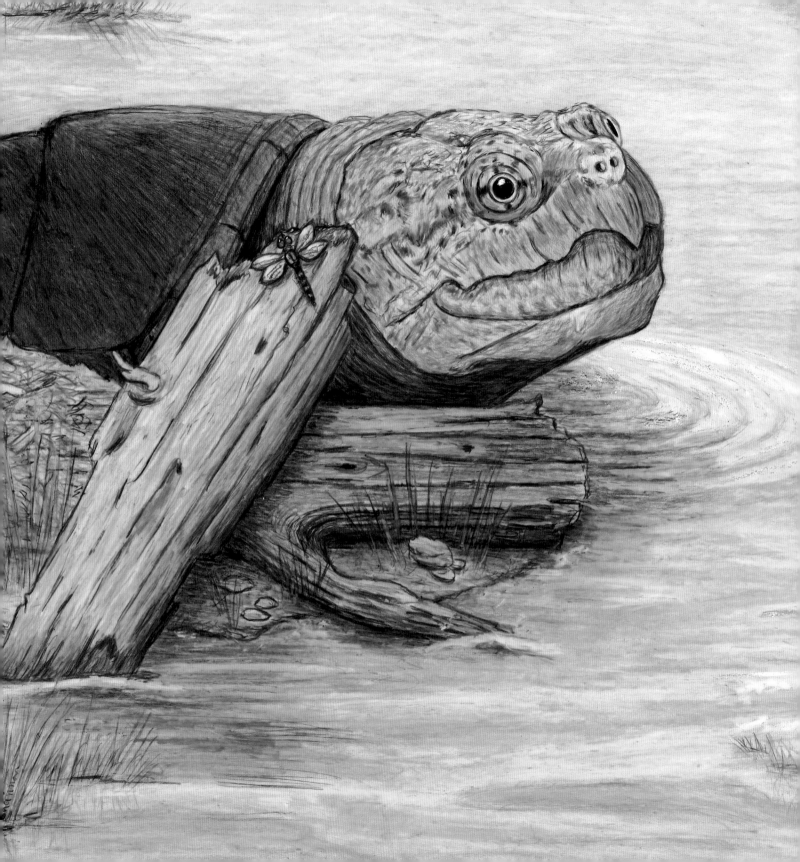

The chick's webbed feet made ripples as they kicked. Nearby, a hungry snapping turtle noticed them. Quietly, he closed in.

While looking for minnows underwater, the mother loon saw the turtle. Surfacing quickly and crying out, she beat her white-spotted black wings against the water. Then she rushed toward the turtle. Frightened, it forgot the chick.

Having heard his mother's danger signal, the loon chick had sped to shore. He had reached a spot between some cattails and a tree branch that had fallen partway into the lake. Silently, he waited in the water, hiding under the branch. Until his mother or father came, he wouldn't move. No matter what.

The mother loon's angry wailing stopped. She had scared off the turtle. Now, the chick knew, she would come looking for him. His father, off fishing in another part of the lake, would have heard the noises too and would also be searching.

Soon, something began splashing loudly nearby. Could it be the loon chick's mother? He peeked around the branch. But it was a raccoon, washing a few blueberries before eating them.

Quickly, the chick ducked back into hiding. It was too late. The raccoon had seen the tiny loon. He was about to pounce when—

Whump!

A huge hoof came down, just missing one of the raccoon's back paws. A thirsty cow moose had come to drink and wasn't watching where she stepped. Because of his splashing, the raccoon hadn't noticed her slow, quiet approach.

The moose snorted at the raccoon as he tried to dodge her wide hooves. The cow's next step accidentally pinched the tip of his tail. Chattering with anger, the raccoon dashed up the bank. He'd find supper somewhere else.

Lowering her shaggy brown head, the moose drank with loud slurps. Then she turned to the branch in the water, tearing off shreds of bark with her strong teeth.

Munching, she ambled off, almost squashing the loon chick.
The moose didn't hear his tiny peeps of fear.

As the big animal's footsteps faded into the forest, silence
returned to the lake shore, and the chick rested.

What was that? Something was moving on top of the bank. Something was coming—fast—toward the chick's hiding place.

A sleek, brown otter slithered down the bank. Just ahead of her, a large, green bullfrog dove into the water with one powerful jump.

The frog made a sharp turn, darting through the tiny loon's hiding place. Never taking her eyes off her prey, the otter swam swiftly under the branch, too. She never saw the motionless chick, which she gladly would have eaten instead of the frog.

Soon, all was quiet once again

"Ahhooo! Ahhooo!" That was the adult loons' "Where are you?" call. The chick wanted to answer but didn't. If another raccoon or otter heard him before a parent was close enough to protect him…

In time, the sun began to set. It turned the dark red of a loon's eyes. The shadows deepened until the chick's dark gray down was almost invisible.

He shivered in the cool evening air. It was a tiny movement but enough for another pair of watchful eyes to see. Red eyes. His mother's eyes.

"Kwuk, kwuk." That was the loon's way of saying, "It's safe. Come."
Happily the chick paddled through the cattails to join her. Little
by little, the adult bird sank into the cold water until he could
scramble onto her back. Snuggling down into her black and white
feathers, the chick warmed his chilly feet.

The mother loon called softly to her mate as she swam. Soon, the family was together again.

Fun Facts About Loons

You've probably heard of birds that can't fly—like the ostrich. But did you know there is a kind of bird that can't walk? Loons! Their legs are so far back on their bodies that they're off balance when they try to stand. On land, they lie on their chests and push themselves along with their feet, slowly and awkwardly.

So it's not surprising that loons spend most of their time in the water. Their legs are placed just right for swimming and diving. Common loons (the type in this book) may hold their breath for three minutes and go down dozens or even hundreds of feet beneath the surface.

Another place loons spend a lot of time is the air. But taking off isn't easy for them. They have to splash along on top of the water for as much as four hundred yards—the same as four football fields—flapping their wings as hard as possible. Once they get airborne, though, they can fly at more than sixty miles an hour—the same speed as a car on the highway. Each year, loons from Maine fly south for thousands of miles to spend the winter in the ocean off Florida's coast.

Since they're so at home in the water and air, why do loons spend any time on the ground? It's because they must build a nest. For about a month, the mother and father loon take turns keeping the one or two eggs in their nest warm.

Just a few hours after loon chicks hatch, they're swimming or riding on their parents' backs. A few weeks later, they begin diving to catch small fish for themselves. Before they are three months old, they fly south for the winter. And they make this long trip without their parents, who leave first! Somehow, the young loons know just where to go.